C901021511

D1577089

libraries ni

You can renew your book at any library or online at
www.librariesni.org.uk

If you require help please email - enquiries@librariesni.org.uk

Jack the Giant Killer

Malachy Doyle and Graham Philpot

W
FRANKLIN WATTS
LONDON•SYDNEY

Chapter 1:
The Hungry Giant

Once upon a time, when good King Arthur ruled the land, there was a huge and horrible giant in the county of Cornwall. His name was Cormoran. He lived in a cave on the island of Saint Michael's Mount, and he was massive!

Because he was so big, it meant he was always hungry. And because he was always hungry, it meant he didn't care too much what he ate. Cows or hogs, sheep or dogs – Cormoran would eat just about anything.

He'd never been known to eat people, but what was going to happen when there were no animals left?

Every few nights, the enormous giant would come striding through the waves from Saint Michael's Mount. **"I need food!"** he'd roar.

Everyone ran, screaming and yelling, into their houses, barring the doors and bolting the windows. Any animals that were forgotten in the rush to escape the clutches of the ravenous giant were never seen again – cats or dogs, horses or donkeys.

Chapter 2:
The Brave Boy

However there was one boy, and his name was Jack, who wasn't afraid.

"I've had enough of that monster, eating all our animals and scaring all our people! He ate my precious pig last night, and that's the final straw!" he declared.

"Yes, but what are you going to do about it?" said the others.

"I'm going to sort out that great bully, once and for all!" cried Jack.

So that night, when everyone was sleeping, Jack crept out of the house, with his spade in one hand and his horn in the other.

He waited until low tide and then, by the light of the moon, he picked his way across the rocks to Saint Michael's Mount.

9

When he got to the giant's lair, Jack started digging a hole in the ground at the mouth of the cave. It took the best part of the night, for it had to be a really massive hole, three times as deep as Jack himself.

When he'd finally made it deep enough
he covered it over with sticks and
soil and then a load of straw,
so you wouldn't even know
it was there!

Chapter 3:
To Catch a Giant

Jack waited on the far side of the hole and, as the sun peeped over the horizon, he pulled out his horn and he blew it.

"PAAARRRRRP!"
"Who's making all that noise? I'm
trying to sleep!" roared the terrible giant
from inside the cave.

But was Jack scared? No, he was not.

So he blew his horn again, even louder.

"PAAARRRRRP!"

"**If you don't stop now, whoever you are,**" roared the giant, "**I'll come out there and eat you for breakfast!**"

Taking care to go round the side of the hole, Jack marched right up to the door of the cave, where Cormoran was sure to see him, and blew even louder still.

"PAAARRRRRP!"

17

"Right!" boomed the mighty giant. **"I warned you!"**

This time Jack turned and ran, all the way back to the other side of the hole. Cormoran bounded up and out of his cave, and he was just about to grab hold of poor Jack and rip off his tiny head, when ...

19

Chapter 3:
Into the Pit

"**Aaarrrggghhh!**" yelled
the giant, crashing through the sticks and
the straw, and dropping deep down to the
bottom of the newly-dug pit.

Before Cormoran could do a thing about it, the boy grabbed his spade, took a mighty swing and whacked the mighty monster on the head.

"Bongggggg!"

"**Aaarrrggghhh!**" yelled the giant again, reaching out an arm to grab hold of Jack and pull him into the hole.

But the quick-footed boy skipped out of his
way, swung the spade and whacked the
mighty fellow one more time, full-force on
the other side of his head.

"Bonggggg!"

The giant whimpered, and then went silent.
"That's what you get for eating my pig!"
cried Jack.

He ran around the hole, whooping and skipping. "I've done it!" he yelled. "I've saved the village, and all the people, and all the remaining animals!"

He tippy-toed into the giant's cave to see what he could find. Bats flew around his face, bones crunched under his feet, and he didn't like it in there, not one bit. But there was a faint light, leading him right to the very back, and when Jack got there, he made out the shape of an old wooden chest.

The light seemed to be coming from inside, and when he lifted the lid, he couldn't believe his eyes. It was full to the brim with gold and silver! "Treasure!" gasped Jack.

Chapter 5:
Home Again

It was a long hard pull home to the village. But when Jack got back, dragging the giant along by one hand and the treasure chest along by the other, everyone was amazed.

They lifted him up on their shoulders,
then, and paraded him through the village.
"Hurrah!" they yelled. "Hurrah for Jack the
Giant Killer!"
And that's what they called him, from that
day on.

So they made him a
sword and they made
him a shield, and on
it was written:
"Here's the bravest
Cornish man, who
killed the giant
Cormoran!"
And Jack wore it
proudly, for the rest
of his days.

About the story

Jack the Giant Killer is an English fairy tale which was included by Joseph Jacobs in his collection *English Fairy Tales* in 1890.

Sir Thomas Malory also tells a story about a giant – at Mont Saint Michel (a castle in Brittany, France) rather than Saint Michael's Mount in Cornwall. Malory's story tells of King Arthur defeating a child-eating giant and was published in *Le Mort d'Arthur* (The Death of Arthur) in 1485.

There are many giants in Cornish, Welsh, Norse and Breton mythology. Young Jack from this story goes on to kill many more giants, usually by coming up with a clever plan to outwit them.

Be in the story!

Imagine you live in Jack's village. Design a "WANTED" poster for the giant. Remember to include why he needs to be stopped and what reward is offered.

Now imagine that you are Jack. You are giving an interview about your adventure. Don't forget to tell everyone just how brave you were!

First published in 2014 by
Franklin Watts
338 Euston Road
London
NW1 3BH

Franklin Watts Australia
Level 17/207 Kent Street
Sydney
NSW 2000

Text © Malachy Doyle 2014
Illustrations © Graham Philpot 2014
All rights reserved.

The rights of Malachy Doyle to be identified as the author
and Graham Philpot to be identified as the illustrator
of this Work have been asserted in accordance with the
Copyright, Designs and Patents Act, 1988.

A CIP catalogue record for this book is available
from the British Library.

The artwork for this story first appeared in
Hopscotch Adventures: Jack the Giant-Killer

ISBN 978 1 4451 2997 6 (hbk)
ISBN 978 1 4451 2998 3 (pbk)
ISBN 978 1 4451 3000 2 (library ebook)
ISBN 978 1 4451 2999 0 (ebook)

Series Editor: Jackie Hamley
Series Advisor: Catherine Glavina
Series Designer: Cathryn Gilbert

Printed in China

Franklin Watts is a divison of
Hachette Children's Books,
an Hachette UK company.
www.hachette.co.uk